Asian Folktales Retold

Indonesian Fables of Feats and Fortunes

Told and Edited by Kuniko Sugiura

Illustrated by Koji Honda
Translated by Matthew Galgani
Executive Editor: Miyoko Matsutani

The Mischievous Mouse Deer, Kanchil   3
Panji Kuraras and His Champion Rooster   14
The Water Buffalo That Saved the Nation   26

HEIAN

Hearing Tales as They Are Told

Do you love to listen to stories? I do. Can you listen really well?

For hundreds of years, people have passed down folktales from grandparents and parents to children by telling—not writing—them.

When people tell you a story, you don't just hear with your ears. You learn a lot from the voices the storytellers use, how they move their arms, legs, head, shoulders, and body, the expressions on their face—all the tools they use to make their tales come alive.

This book, and the others in the series Asian Folktales Retold, was created to help you truly "hear" Asian folktales and understand them deeply.

As you listen to these tales, or perhaps read them yourself when you're older, figure out for yourself what they mean. If you can hear the storyteller's voice in your head, then you are listening really well.

Published by HEIAN, P.O. Box 8208, Berkeley, California 94707
HEIAN is an imprint of Stone Bridge Press
www.stonebridge.com • sbp@stonebridge.com

© 2001 Kuniko Sugiura and Koji Honda
Originally published in Japan by Hoshinowakai

Printed in China

LIBRARY OF CONGRESS CATALOGING-IN-PUBLICATION DATA

Sugiura, Kuniko, 1943–
    [Katari obasan no Indonesia minwa. English. Selections]
    Indonesian fables of feats and fortunes / told and edited by Kuniko Sugiura; illustrated by Koji Honda; translated by Matthew Galgani; executive editor Miyoko Matsutani.
       v. cm.—(Asian folktales retold)
    "Originally published in Japan by Hoshinowakai"—Copyright p.
    Summary: Three Indonesian folktales, one of a small deer who tricks an alligator, one of a rooster who helps his master find his true home, and one of a baby water buffalo that goes into battle to save the people of Sumatra.
    Contents: The mischievous mouse deer, Kanchil—Panji Kuraras and his champion rooster—The water buffalo that saved the nation.
    ISBN-13: 978-0-89346-950-4 (hardcover)
    1. Tales—Indonesia. [1. Folklore—Indonesia.] I. Honda, Koji, 1962– ill. II. Galgani, Matthew. III. Matsutani, Miyoko, 1926– IV. Title.
    PZ8.1.S943Inc 2007
    398.2—dc22
    [E]

2006033773

The Mischievous Mouse Deer, Kanchil

In Indonesia, there is an animal about half the size of a small deer. It is called a kanchil, which means mouse deer. The kanchil in this story is very clever and likes to play tricks.

One day, a very long time ago, a kanchil was running through the forest.

"I'm so fast," the kanchil thought, "that no one can outrun me. Even if a tiger tried to catch me, I'd be long gone in a split second." These thoughts put him in such a good mood that he didn't notice he had run right out of the forest.

In front of him flowed a river. On the far shore, the kanchil spotted a forest he had never seen before.

"I'd like to check that forest out," he thought, but he didn't know how to swim. As he wondered whether he could find a way across the river, he noticed an alligator napping in the water.

"Aha!" he thought. "I have an idea that just might work." He called out, "Mr. Alligator, Mr. Alligator, please wake up."

Slowly lifting a sleepy eyelid, the alligator looked up at the kanchil.

"Say, Mr. Alligator, you sure are big," said the kanchil. "But you probably don't have any friends. You're here all by yourself, right?"

"Nope," the alligator replied lazily. "I have lots of friends."

"Is that so? But I'm sure you don't have as many friends as we kanchils do."

"Don't be so sure," said the alligator. "I have a bunch of friends right here in this river."

"Really?" asked the kanchil. "Show me how many, and I'll count them for you."

The alligator, by now fully awake, called out to his friends, and in an instant a whole swarm of alligators appeared. Seeing their huge mouths and sharp teeth, the kanchil became a little frightened, but he pretended not to be scared and said to the alligators, "Wow! There really are a lot of you. Why don't you line up from here to the other side of the river, so I can count how many."

The alligators lined up, forming what looked like a long, brown bridge.

"Ready?" asked the kanchil. "I'm about to count you, so don't move."

With that, the kanchil stepped onto the back of the closest alligator. He counted as he hopped from one alligator's back to the next. "One, two, three, four, five . . ."

When he reached the other side, he turned to the alligators and laughed. "Ha, ha, ha! All I really wanted to do was cross to the other side. So, thanks for building a bridge for me!"

Then the kanchil ran off to explore the forest he had never seen before.

Well, the alligator was angry that he had been tricked, and he began plotting his revenge. He watched the shore for any sign that the kanchil was coming back. Sure enough, after a while, he spotted the kanchil, who was thirsty and had come to the river for a drink.

As soon as the kanchil put his hoof in the water, he let out a scream of pain. The alligator had clamped his teeth onto the kanchil's leg.

"Uh-oh, I'm in trouble now!" thought the kanchil, but he put his mind to work. Then, very calmly, he said, "Mr. Alligator, my friend, unfortunately that thing you're biting is a branch of a tree. If it's my leg you want to bite, it's over here." And the kanchil shook a nearby branch to show the alligator.

Well, the alligator let go of the kanchil and lunged for the branch. The kanchil quickly pulled his leg out of the water and turned to mock the alligator, saying, "Thanks for letting me go, my alligator friend. Now go chew on that branch for a while!" And off the kanchil ran again.

Tricked a second time, the alligator was seething with anger. To get revenge, he decided to go ashore and spy on the kanchil by posing as an old, broken tree trunk. As soon as the kanchil came close, the alligator planned to swallow him whole.

After a little while, the kanchil came back to the water for a drink again. When he saw something strange sticking out of the ground, he realized right away that it was the alligator, and he just had to tease him again.

"Is that an old, broken tree trunk I see?" asked the kanchil in a loud voice. "Or could it be an alligator? If it's just a tree trunk, then I'm fine. But if it's an alligator, then I'm really in danger. How can I tell which it is? I guess if it's a big, strong alligator, then it can stand up forever. But if it's an old tree, then it will soon fall over."

What do you think happened? Sure enough, the alligator fell over—and even did a couple of somersaults.

"Ha, ha, ha, silly alligator," the kanchil chuckled. "Now tell me, in what country do trees do somersaults? Ha, ha, ha, ha!" And the kanchil galloped away.

Well, the kanchil had had so much fun fooling the alligator that he wanted to play more tricks. "Next time, I think I'll fool a tiger, the strongest beast in the jungle," he decided.

One day soon after, the kanchil, looking mischievous as usual, was sitting under a rhus tree. (Do you know that tree? Well, its ripe fruit is shaped like an egg and is extremely sour.)

Just then, a tiger came by and asked the kanchil what he was doing.

"Actually, Mr. Tiger, I've been appointed guardian of the royal eggs," the kanchil said. "These are extraordinarily delicious eggs that only the king himself is allowed to eat, so I've been told to make sure that no one takes them."

"Won't you let me have one?" asked the tiger.

"Absolutely not. The king would kill me if I did that."

"But you have so many," argued the tiger. "Surely the king wouldn't miss just one. . . . Well, I guess if I can't have an egg, I'll have to eat you instead."

"Wait, wait," cried the kanchil. "Don't be in such a hurry. I have an idea. I'll go far away to escape the king's anger, and, when I give you the word, go ahead and eat an egg."

With that, the kanchil galloped away and hid behind a large tree. "You can eat one now," he yelled.

The tiger immediately grabbed the largest piece of fruit and took a big bite.

"Aiiieeeee, it's sour!" he screamed. The fruit made the tiger's mouth numb, and he wasn't able to eat anything for quite a while.

Well, of course, he became very angry at the kanchil. "If I ever see that kanchil again, I'll get him back for this," the tiger growled.

When he walked back into the jungle, he suddenly noticed the kanchil hiding in the hole of a tree.

"Come on out, Mr. Kanchil, so I can eat you," the tiger barked.

"W-w-wait a second," stuttered the kanchil. "I'm guarding the king's drum. The king will be here any second now, so please wait until he gets here. As soon as I return the king's drum, you have every right to eat me."

"Hmmm, the king's drum? I'd like to beat the king's drum," thought the tiger. So he made the kanchil an offer.

"Let me beat the drum," said the tiger, "and I'll let you go."

"That's im-im-impossible!" said the kanchil in a worried voice. "If I do that, the king will kill me. So, either way I'm going to die!"

"I just want to beat the drum a little," said the tiger. "After that, I promise I'll never eat you."

"OK, then," said the kanchil, "I have an idea. I'll go away where the king can't see me, and, when I give the word, you can beat the drum. It's hanging right here."

With that, the kanchil galloped away and hid behind a large tree.

"You can beat the drum now," he yelled to the tiger.

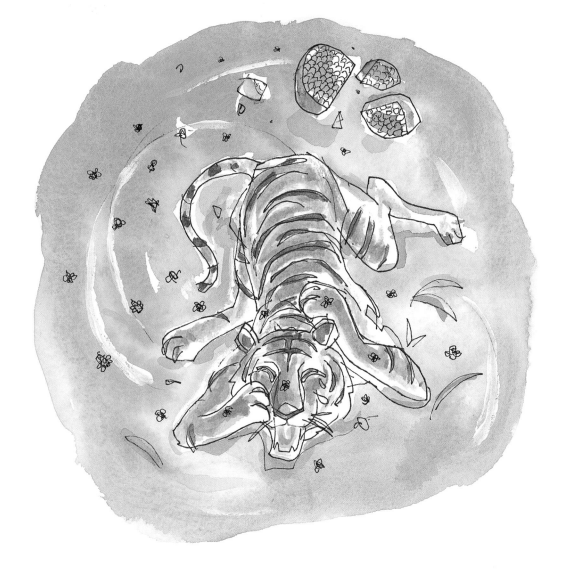

The tiger quickly took down the drum and started beating it. It made quite a lovely sound . . . but . . . it wasn't really a drum—it was a carpenter bees' nest! So, the more the tiger beat it, the angrier these huge bees got, until they rushed out and started stinging him. The tiger yelled and yowled and ran for his life. But no matter how far or how fast he ran, the carpenter bees chased him, stinging him over and over.

Meanwhile, the kanchil galloped off peacefully, deep into the forest.

And that's the end of the story of the mischievous mouse deer known as a kanchil.

Panji Kuraras
and His Champion Rooster

Once upon a time, long, long ago, there was a king who had only one son. To help the prince grow up to be a great ruler, the king wanted the boy taught well. But no matter how hard his teachers tried, the prince refused to study. He paid no attention to learning manners or martial arts either. Only one thing excited the prince, and that was cockfighting.

Now, I need to tell you that, in Indonesia, roosters that crow at the break of dawn are considered sacred birds. Still, the people in those olden days liked cockfights—where they watched two roosters fight each other. The fighting roosters were called "gamecocks," and sometimes their owners attached sharp blades or needles to their toenails. Then the birds fought until one lost its will to go on. This was the custom long, long ago. Today, most people know that cockfights are cruel because they harm the roosters, and in many countries cockfighting is against the law.

Well, the prince devoted all his attention to gathering the strongest roosters and watching them fight. Finally, the king grew tired of trying to educate his son, and he banished the prince from the palace—sent him away and would not let him return. In fact, the king was so angry that he banished the prince from the whole country.

What was the prince to do? He wandered here and there and became lost in the huge forest between his father's kingdom and the neighboring country. There he met a beautiful young woman. Both her parents had died, and she lived all alone in a little shack in the middle of the forest.

Seeing that the prince was tired and hungry, the young woman fed him and gently took care of him. Since the prince had nowhere else to go, he stayed with the young woman in the forest. Soon, the two were married and living happily together.

One day, rumors of the king's death reached as far away as this huge forest. The prince suddenly became restless and wanted to return to the palace. Since he was the king's only son, he thought, he could now go back and become king.

"I'm going home," the prince said to the young woman, "but I can't take you with me."

His wife was shocked. "Please take me with you," she cried.

But the prince refused, and he left the forest alone. He headed straight for the palace.

Abandoned by her husband, the young woman sat under a large tree and wept. She knew she would soon give birth to the prince's child.

Suddenly, a hawk flew across the sky carrying a little rooster chick in its mouth. When the hawk was right above the young woman, it unexpectedly let go of the chick and flew off. The chick landed on the young woman's knee and squealed softly. The kind young woman decided to keep the baby bird.

A short while later, the young woman gave birth to a beautiful little boy. He quickly grew healthy and strong. His only friend was the little bird, and they were together all night and all day. The little bird also grew healthy and strong, turning into a fine rooster with an impressive crest.

Now, this rooster crowed with a most unusual sound. As if singing, the rooster would crow:

Cookoo lookoo cookoo las
My master's Panji Kuraras
He lives with his mother in a forest shack
While his father's in a palace and never looks back

Because of this song, the boy came to be called Panji Kuraras.

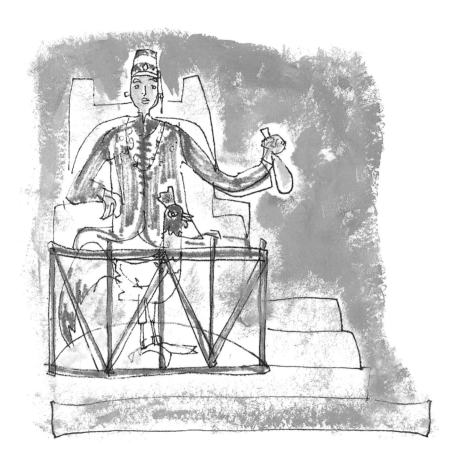

Meanwhile, back in the palace, the prince soon was crowned king. Even though he was supposed to rule the land, he left all the work to his ministers and cared for nothing except cockfighting. All day long, you could hear the screams of the cocks fighting in the palace grounds. In fact, the palace became little more than a cockfighting arena.

In the forest, Panji Kuraras turned nine years old. "Where is my father?" he asked for the first and only time.

His mother looked away and couldn't answer. Panji Kuraras did not ask again.

One day he declared that he wanted to see the city.

"The city is so far away," said his mother, trying to stop him. "And you never know what mean and dangerous people you might meet. There's nothing to harm you here. Please don't go—stay with me."

"Don't worry, Mother," Panji Kuraras replied. "I'll have my rooster with me. I'll try my luck and soon return." And without another word he headed off, with his rooster at his side.

When they arrived in the city, they headed straight for the palace. "My rooster challenges the king's gamecocks," Panji Kuraras yelled in his loudest voice.

The crowd inside the palace was surprised at Panji Kuraras and his rooster. "Who is this mere boy," they thought, "who dares to challenge the king?"

But the king was curious and accepted the match. He was happy to meet a child who was interested in cockfighting.

"If my rooster loses, I'll give you this," the king said, holding out the bag of gold he was betting. "But what will you give me if you lose?"

"I'll work as the keeper of your roosters." The king looked at Panji Kuraras and had a strange feeling that he had met this boy somewhere. But before he could remember when and where, it was time for the cockfight to begin.

The king's rooster had sharp knives attached to its toenails. Panji Kuraras's rooster had no blades. How could it possibly win?

Within seconds, the fight was over. And the fallen rooster was the king's!

Panji Kuraras's rooster began to crow its song.

Cookoo lookoo cookoo las
My master's Panji Kuraras
He lives with his mother in a forest shack
While his father's in a palace and never looks back

While the palace crowd stood still in shock, Panji Kuraras and his rooster took the bag of gold and quickly headed home.

His mother was relieved to see him and the rooster safe. But the next day, the boy and his rooster returned to the palace.

This time, the king chose an even stronger rooster from his flock. The people in the crowd were excited and began placing their own bets on the fight. Some were rooting for the king; others for Panji Kuraras.

Once again, Panji Kuraras's rooster defeated the king's rooster in a single move. And again it began to crow as if it were singing.

Cookoo lookoo cookoo las
My master's Panji Kuraras
He lives with his mother in a forest shack
While his father's in a palace and never looks back

This time, Panji Kuraras brought home even more gold. But his mother was not happy. "Never go there again," she pleaded.

"Let me go just once more, Mother."

The next morning, Panji Kuraras and his rooster headed for the palace again. The king was waiting with his fiercest rooster. Steely eyes, razor-sharp beak, terrifying nails—there was no telling how many other roosters' lives it had destroyed.

"What are you placing as your bet today?" the king asked.

"My neck," replied Panji Kuraras.

"Splendid!" said the king. "I admire your courage." Then the king showed a bag of gold several times larger than the others he had bet before.

All the people in the palace held their breath as the two roosters were released into the ring. The battle was intense, but, sure enough, Panji Kuraras's rooster was victorious. And, once again, it began to crow as if singing;

Cookoo lookoo cookoo las
My master's Panji Kuraras
He lives with his mother in a forest shack
While his father's in a palace and never looks back

The king took a long look at Panji Kuraras's face. He was sure he had seen this boy before, but for the life of him he couldn't remember where.

"Tell me who your parents are and where you live," the king said.

"I have no father," replied Panji Kuraras. "I live in a shack in the forest with my mother and my rooster." Then he headed home.

Unable to shake the strange feeling that he had met Panji Kuraras before, the king secretly followed the boy home.

Panji Kuraras and his rooster made their way to the forest and went deep into the woods, until they came to the little shack.

"Mother!" Panji Kuraras yelled, "My rooster won again today! And neither one of us is hurt at all."

The face of the woman at the shack lit up, and she hugged Panji Kuraras.

When the king saw her face, he remembered everything in an instant—and he realized that Panji Kuraras was his son. But as the king approached the boy and his mother, the mother froze with fear. Then the king gently took the hand of his wife, and they both began to weep.

The king felt the deepest shame for all that he had done. He begged his wife and son for forgiveness and asked them to come live with him in the palace.

So, off to the palace they went, Panji Kuraras now a prince, and his mother now a queen. And there they lived together happily, parents and child.

In time, Panji Kuraras became king, and he ruled his kingdom justly.

And that's the end of the story of Panji Kuraras and his victorious rooster.

The Water Buffalo
That Saved the Nation

In a western region of the large Indonesian island of Sumatra lives a group of people known as Minangkabau. "Minang" means to win, and "kabau" means water buffalo. In this region, water buffalo are considered sacred, and the roofs of buildings are shaped like buffalo horns. Tools and other handmade things are often designed with a water buffalo design. So, how did these people come to be called Minangkabau—victorious water buffalo? Here's the story.

Once upon a time, a tranquil and comfortable nation lived on the western side of the island of Sumatra. The people worked hard and had no shortage of food, clothing, and shelter. Everything about their life and land was peaceful.

On the neighboring island of Java was a large nation with a strong army.

One day, a messenger from the king of Java arrived on Sumatra with a demand:

"Become the subjects of the king of Java, and do what he says. Or face destruction from his powerful army. Which shall it be?"

What could the peaceful people do? With no army to speak of, they would soon be crushed if they went to war. Yet they couldn't stand the thought of having to follow orders from the king of Java.

As they wondered what to do, a very wise man suddenly had an idea: Why not choose one water buffalo from each country and have them do battle to decide which country would win?

Everyone thought that it was an excellent idea. But could they convince the king of Java to agree? They chose a very persuasive speaker and sent him to the king.

"If we fight a war," he told the king, "even the winner will suffer great losses. And while we are fighting each other, who's to say that another nation won't attack us both? So, rather than have our people fight each other, why don't we have our water buffalo do the fighting for us? If our buffalo loses, we will do as you demanded and follow your orders. If our water buffalo wins, then you will leave us alone forever."

"A most interesting suggestion," the king said to himself. "This means I can take over an entire nation without lifting a finger!" Java was a large kingdom, and he knew it had no shortage of powerful water buffalo. The king could hardly keep from laughing as he thought about how he would soon conquer an entire nation with a single water buffalo!

So, the king accepted the idea immediately and rounded up an unbelievably large and powerful water buffalo.

When the people of Sumatra saw it, they were very discouraged and sad. Their own water buffalo were smart, but it would be very tough to defeat such an impressive beast.

"Don't worry," said the same wise man who had come up with the idea. "Here's what we need to do: Take a newborn water buffalo calf and separate it from its mother for three days, giving it no milk. Then we'll let the calf fight the king's water buffalo, and it will win."

The people only half-believed in this plan, but since they couldn't come up with anything better they agreed to follow the wise man's advice.

When the day of the battle came, the large, fierce water buffalo from Java and the baby water buffalo from Sumatra were brought to the fighting grounds. You couldn't help but feel sorry for the calf, who seemed clearly no match for the huge buffalo.

When the people released the ropes holding both animals, the calf, who hadn't had any milk in three days, charged straight at the large water buffalo. Looking for milk to drink, the calf butted its head right into the other animal's stomach. Well, guess what? A sharp knife, called a "kris," had been attached to the calf's horns, and it poked right into the huge water buffalo's soft underbelly. Squealing in pain, the king's water buffalo ran away.

The people of western Sumatra were thrilled and relieved!

"This certainly did not turn out the way I expected," said the king of Java. "But a promise is a promise." He also could see that, if he ever went to war with such smart and clever people, he would, indeed, pay a big price. He vowed right then never again to threaten this small but great nation.

And that is the end of the tale about the victorious baby water buffalo who saved the Minangkabau nation.

About the Series and This Book

The Asian Folktales Retold series was created to capture the spirit of Asian folktales and give them new life, showing children how these stories help us both evaluate the modern world and connect with a rich cultural past. The stories strive to preserve the oral flavor of recountings of tales passed down for generations, and they are intended to be read aloud to experience the full joy of this picture book.

Like all folktales, the stories in this book have been passed down verbally, but because Indonesia is peopled by so many ethnic groups, they were told in different languages and versions in different regions. This book gathers highly popular stories that a visitor living in Jakarta for just a few years would come to know.

About the Storyteller and Editor

When Kuniko Sugiura was born, in 1943 in Aichi Prefecture, Japan, her father was in Indonesia, and she developed a lifelong love for and interest in that country. Sugiura graduated from Aichi Prefectural University and became involved in telling folktales through her work with children's books.

Sugiura's granddaughter was 20 months old when the author's son-in-law was transferred to a job in Indonesia, and his family moved there. Sugiura loved singing lullabies, reciting nursery rhymes, and telling fairy tales to her grandchild in Japanese, but when she visited the family in Indonesia she developed an interest in sharing Indonesian folktales with the child, too. She asked her daughter for the Indonesian stories children liked best and told those to her granddaughter. She also turned to Internet sources and print collections for Indonesian folklore.

After studying folktales in the course of her travels, Sugiura researched how these stories are currently told and experienced. She has written and edited several Japanese-language books on folklore and storytelling and is an active member of many folklore associations.

About the Illustrator

Born in 1962 in Ishikawa Prefecture, Japan, artist Koji Honda graduated with a degree in sculpture from the Kanazawa College of Art. From 1985 to 1993, he worked at Maeda Outdoor Arts Design, designing monuments, sculptures, and other works. In 1997, he illustrated and oversaw the design of the five-volume series Biotope de Asobo (Having Fun with Biotope), published by Hoshinowakai. Since 1999, Honda's artworks have been included in several exhibitions.

About Indonesia

Indonesia is made up of almost 18,000 islands. Some are very large, like Java, Sumatra, and Borneo, but many others are tiny, and more than 7,000 are uninhabited. The islands stretch about 3,000 miles from east to west, forming the world's largest archipelago nation.

Most of the country is in the southern hemisphere, but part crosses the equator and extends into the northern hemisphere. The population is more than 200 million and includes 250 to 300 ethnic groups, who speak more than 300 languages.

From infancy, babies hear and learn a native ethnic language. Once in school, children learn to speak Indonesian, the common language that the people use to communicate across ethnic groups.

Indonesia's people vary widely in the way they look—with a range of skin colors, eye shapes, and hair colors and textures. While the majority of Indonesians are Muslim, a variety of religions and ways of thinking are found among the islands' peoples.

Each ethnic group has its unique customs and culture, passed down from the days long before Indonesia was unified as a country. One important way traditions pass from generation to generation is in folktales.

Other Books from Heian

Asian Folktales Retold

VIETNAM

Told and Edited by Masao Sakairi

Illustrated by Shoko Kojima

Vietnamese Fables of Frogs and Toads

The Frog Bride, The Toad Who Brought the Rain

ISBN-13: 978-0-89346-947-4

Vietnamese Tales of Rabbits and Watermelons

The Rabbit Who Always Got Away, Mai An-Tiem and the Watermelons

ISBN-13: 978-0-89346-948-1

CHINA

Told by Miwa Kurita

Illustrated by Saoko Mitsukuri

China Tells How the World Began!

How the World Began, Why Cats Hate Rats

ISBN-13: 978-0-89346-944-3

Chinese Fables Remembered

The Brothers and the Birds, The Two Rooster Friends

ISBN-13: 978-0-89346-945-0

Each volume $16.95, hardcover